Songbird and other stories

JENNIFER LAMONT LEO

Songbird and Other Stories by Jennifer Lamont Leo
Published by Mountain Majesty Media, Inc.
PO Box 638, Cocolalla, ID 83813

ISBN-13: 978-1-7337058-1-3

For more information on this book and the author, visit
www.jenniferlamontleo.com

These stories are works of fiction. Names, characters, and
incidents are all products of the author's imagination or are used
for fictional purposes. Any mentioned brand names, places, and
trademarks remain the property of their respective owners, bear
no association with the author or the publisher, and are used for
fictional purposes only.

Library of Congress Cataloging-in-Publication Data
Leo, Jennifer Lamont
Songbird and Other Stories / Jennifer Lamont Leo 1st ed.

Other books by Jennifer Lamont Leo

You're the Cream in My Coffee

Ain't Misbehavin'

CONTENTS

Songbird

Chicago, 1928

"Ladies and gentlemen, let's hear one more song from the incomparable Miss Dot Rodgers."

As the bandleader signaled and the trumpeter swung into the final number, I discreetly blotted my damp forehead with a hankie, then smiled and grasped the microphone. Electric fans whirring in the dark corners of the room did little to dispel the steamy, smoky air and bring relief to the perspiring patrons, now dwindled to just a handful of tables. One group of out-of-towners cheered, determined to get their money's worth by staying out all night. I was eager to finish the set, the last one of the evening. Just one more song and then Louie would drive me home in his Packard convertible, top down, cool night breezes caressing my face and hair as we sped through the dark Chicago streets. We had a deal: the band could play all night if they felt like it, but my shift ended at two sharp. Morning came early for a girl who sold hats at Marshall Field. Maybe someday singing would be my full-time gig. But until then, two a.m. was my limit.

Crooning the opening lyrics of "Carolina," I glanced through the haze to where Louie stood at the bar, talking with a redheaded waitress. The new one. Carla, or maybe Marla–I couldn't remember. The same one he'd been talking to practically all evening. My gut tightened. Surely he wasn't interested in that girl as anything more than a new employee. He was just being nice, the boss making the new kid feel welcome.

Trouble was, Louie's interest frequently went further. This girl wasn't the first to draw his attention and, much as I wished I could deny it, she wouldn't be the last.

At the start of the second verse, I forced myself to look away and flung a brilliant smile toward the tableful of conventioneers, trying to ignore the burning sensation in my chest. *Don't make a bigger deal out of it than it is,* I reminded myself sternly. Not so long ago, I'd been that new girl, washing dishes upstairs in the restaurant, before Louie heard me sing and brought me down to perform in the speakeasy tucked away in the basement. The audience liked what they heard. Now I had a regular gig: three nights a week, ten until two. Decent tips from the butter-and-egg men who appreciated a pretty girl with a voice. By "pretty" I just mean what I'd been told all my life. My hair and eyes are dark and my skin pale. Some called it a strong resemblance to the actress Louise Brooks. My father called it a curse that set me on the road to ruin.

More about him later.

It wasn't always easy to deliver a sparkling performance after being on my feet all day at the department store, but I did my best because I loved to sing. And because I loved Louie–or thought I did. He was certainly a looker: tall, dark-haired, always impeccably dressed, with an easy laugh. And I was grateful to him for giving me the opportunity to sing professionally, even if it was in a basement speakeasy. It could lead to bigger and better things, was what he said, and he should know. He knew lots of people. Sooner or later, a connection would be made that would benefit my musical career. I just needed patience.

Sometimes he acted like he loved me too. He treated me special, bought me expensive gifts, took me to swanky nightspots on my nights off. But he never promised anything. And then there was his roving eye. First there'd been that blonde with the diamond necklace. He'd been forced to pay attention to her, he said, because she was a rich backer of his business interests, whatever that meant. Next there was the sultry visitor from New Orleans with her long eyelashes and Southern drawl. I wasn't sure what her connection was, but she took up a lot of Louie's time for a few weeks.

But he always boomeranged back to me, eventually, and charmed his way back into my good graces. I never understood quite how he did it. I was no pushover and didn't usually take a shine to people who treated me poorly. I'd had enough of that business growing up. But with Louie, there I'd be, letting his smooth talk and seductive flattery reel me in like a perch on a line. As if his charming wizardry drew me under some kind of magic spell.

And I was getting mighty tired of it.

The song drew to a close. I bowed my head, grateful for the audience's applause.

"Thank you all for coming," I said into the mic. I stole a glance at the bar and felt half relieved, half alarmed to see neither Louie nor the redhead standing there. Perhaps the girl had returned to her duties, and Louie was fetching my coat for the ride home. Except I had no coat on that steamy June night. As I stepped off the stage, the bandleader took over the microphone.

"Ladies and gentlemen, another hand for Miss Dot Rodgers." More polite applause. Then, "Folks, we'll stay and play as long as you want to stay and dance."

The band launched into a peppy number and couples took to the dance floor. I grabbed my purse from behind the bar, then headed for the exit. I nodded to the barrel-chested bouncer and he opened the door for me, glancing around the dank basement hallway to make sure no one was lurking outside who shouldn't be. I climbed the dark, narrow staircase, up two flights, past the "legitimate" Italian restaurant, now closed for the evening, that served as a front for the speakeasy. In the ladies' restroom on the top floor, I lifted the window sash and took a deep, refreshing breath of the star-strewn summer night. Directly below the window was the roof of the restaurant's back porch, used only for storage and delivery. For a moment, I was tempted to crawl out the window, sit on the peaceful roof, drink in the caressing breeze, and put off as long as possible the hard truth I suspected was coming. Instead I splashed my flushed cheeks with cool tap water, freshened my powder and lip rouge, spritzed myself with Chanel No. 5–a gift from Louie–and headed back the way I'd come to the door marked Cleaning Supplies. I rapped my knuckles in a specific pattern and the door cautiously creaked open to admit me.

I glanced around the dim, smoke-hazed room, but Louie was nowhere to be seen.

"Is he in the office?"

The bouncer shrugged.

I threaded through the tables to the small office at the back of the room. No light shone through the crack beneath the closed door. He wasn't in there, unless– A sudden fury seized me. What if he was in there with her, enjoying a tête-à-tête, or worse? Without stopping to knock, I grabbed the doorknob and turned. It didn't budge. I raised my arm, preparing to pound.

"You lookin' for somethin'?"

I whirled toward the gruff male voice, heart slamming against my ribs. Ralph Arnetti, one of Louie's associates, eyed me with steely suspicion. My embarrassed laugh burbled forth, more like a choking noise.

"Jeepers, Ralph, you gave me a start." My hand fluttered to my chest. "Why, no–I mean, I'm just looking for Louie. Have you seen him?" I scanned the dance floor, as if I'd suddenly spot him doing the Charleston. At over six feet tall, he'd be hard to miss.

"I ain't seen him." Ralph scowled down at me. "But I know he don't want nobody poking around his office when he ain't there."

"But I'm not–" I'm not nobody, I started to say. I'm his girl. But I bit it back. If I were Louie's girl, Ralph would know it. Wouldn't he? "But I wasn't . . . poking."

Ralph grunted and positioned himself in front of the door, massive hands folded in front of his pinstripe trousers.

"Well, good night." Piqued at being thought a snoop, I gathered my shredded dignity and swept over to the bar.

"Hi, Sam. You seen Louie?"

"No." Something in the bartender's tone strengthened my already robust suspicions. He avoided my gaze, staring instead with intense interest at the rag he was wiping over the bar. Then he said brightly, "Hey, you sounded good up there tonight."

"Don't change the subject. Where is he?"

The balding man sighed. "He gave the new girl a ride home. Said she had a headache."

The familiar punch slammed my gut.

"I see."

When he finally looked at me, I couldn't stand the sympathy in his eyes. "I'm sure he'll be back soon. Lemme give you a drink while you wait."

I lifted my chin. "No, thanks. I'm not waiting around."

"See you Friday then?"

I nodded mutely, tugging on my gloves, not trusting myself to speak for a moment, lest a string of unladylike cuss words erupt. It was hard to fool Sam, though. Like many bartenders, he had remarkable perception into the workings of the human heart. Gently he said, "Look, Dottie. You want I should call you a cab?"

"Yes, please," I said, fighting to keep my voice void of emotion. "I'll wait upstairs."

"You got it." Sam reached for the telephone mounted on a post. As I exited, the bouncer grunted goodnight. Slowly I climbed the stairs and walked through the darkened restaurant, where a man swished a mop over the floor. I stepped carefully around the wet area.

"'Evening, Carlo." My voice sounded weary to my own ears. Weary and old. Old at twenty-four.

"'Evening, Dottie. Say, I was downstairs a little while ago. Crowd loved you tonight."

"Thanks." Even kind words of praise landed flat as dull tin, if they didn't come from Louie's lips.

Louie's lips.

Tight-throated but dry-eyed, I watched through the front window. Silently I recited the lyrics to one of the newer songs, trying hard to think of anything other than Louie's lips and what they might be doing at this moment.

A taxicab pulled up next to the curb. Carlo opened the door and clicked the lock behind me. I gave the cabbie my address as I slid into the backseat, then sat back and stared unseeing out the window.

Let him have his little escapade. He wouldn't have me to come back to again. I was through.

♫

"I've been telling you for ages, he's not good enough for you," Marjorie said on Thursday after work. She and I sat squished together on the crowded streetcar. "You could get any other man just by snapping your fingers."

"I don't want another man," I snarled. "I just wanted the one I had to start treating me right."

"If he didn't treat you right, then you never really had him, did you?"

I slid my friend a glance. I wasn't accustomed to daydreamy Marjorie coming up with sensible nuggets of wisdom.

"You're right," I said. "And I've come to a decision. I've decided to quit."

"Quit what? Dating Louie?"

"Quit everything. Louie, the Villa Italiana, everything."

Marjorie's brow creased. "You mean you'll quit singing? Don't get me wrong. I'm all in favor of your steering clear of Louie and that awful gin joint, but you love to sing. Won't you miss it?"

"I'll miss it terribly," I said. "But I can't keep singing there if I want to avoid Louie. And I need to avoid him. Otherwise he'll keep seeping back into my life like ... like raw sewage."

"A poetic image." Marjorie wrinkled her nose.

I examined my crimson-painted fingernails. "Obviously we can never go back to being just boss and employee. Once that professional barrier's been crossed ..." I sighed, unwilling to complete the thought. "Anyway, I don't want to see him with other women. And I sure don't want to be anywhere around when he comes crawling back, as he always does."

"But your singing..." Marjorie began.

"If he wants to replace me with Marla or Darla or whoever she is, then he can put her up on stage. Let's see how the crowd likes that. I'd just as soon leave town."

Marjorie glanced upward. "Now you're talking applesauce. But honestly ... you have a wonderful voice. I'll bet that once you're out of that horrible place, God will open up some other opportunity to sing. I'll pray that He does."

"You do that," I said flatly. Marjorie felt comfortable praying. Me, not so much. Growing up under the iron fist of a hypocritical preacher father will do that to you. Not that I didn't believe God existed–I did. But a father like mine makes a person think that the Almighty, too, operates with a frown and a fist and little interest in opening doors for wayward daughters.

Marjorie rested a gentle hand on my forearm. "You don't need Louie, Dot. You're worth more than that. What you need is the ..."

I held up a silencing hand. "No sermons today, please." I knew what she was going to say. She was going to say I needed the Lord, or some such, and I was in no mood to hear it.

She closed her mouth for a moment, then said mildly, "Hey, listen. If you'd seriously like to get out of town, come home with me to Kerryville for the weekend."

This caught my interest. A whole weekend? Miles from Chicago, where Louie couldn't come slithering around with his slick words and bouquets of roses, begging me to forgive him?

"That'd be just the ticket," I blurted. "When do we leave?"

"Tomorrow. It's the only weekend Mrs. Cross will let me have off. Do you think Mrs. Blandings will let you take it off as well?"

"I'll ask her first thing tomorrow. She won't like the short notice, but she owes me a favor."

"What favor?"

"I worked extra days when Isabella was out sick. And sold twice as many hats as she would have in that time. Not that I'm bragging."

"You, brag?" Marjorie gave me a wink. "Never."

I shrugged. "Facts are facts."

She giggled. Then a shadow of doubt crept into her blue eyes. "I'd be thrilled if you came with me, but I'm afraid you might be bored. There's not much to do in Kerryville. It's not exactly a booming metropolis."

"Don't worry about me," I said. "I could use a little boredom right about now."

The streetcar screeched to a halt at our stop. We stepped off the stuffy conveyance and strolled down the maple-shaded sidewalk toward our apartment building. All of a sudden, Marjorie glanced at her wristwatch, gasped, and took off at a trot.

"Hey, where's the fire?" I panted, struggling to keep up with her.

"I can't believe I forgot. I've got a rehearsal tonight at the settlement house. I'll be awfully late if I don't hurry. The concert's on the Fourth of July, the costumes still aren't finished–" She suddenly stopped and grabbed my arm. "Would you come and help out? Please?"

I stared. "Who? Me?"

"It would be such a help. You could corral the children, and–"

"Whoa, Nellie. Stop right there. I don't know the first thing about working with children."

"What is there to know? You can help them with their singing. They could use a few pointers."

"Afraid not, doll."

Marjorie picked up the pace again. "Why not?"

"Well . . . it's a church thing, isn't it?"

"Our church helps support the settlement house, yes. But it's for the good of the whole community. What difference does it make?"

I snorted. "I'm sure church people won't be thrilled to have a torch singer teaching their children how to sing."

"Nobody will care. We're desperate."

"Gee, thanks."

Marjorie yanked open the front door of the building and stepped into the tiled vestibule. "You know what I mean. Please?"

"Sorry, sweetie. I have an appointment with a cool bath tonight, and then I'll have to pack if we're going to Kerryville tomorrow."

Marjorie pouted a little, but she let the matter drop.

The next morning, the negotiation with Mrs. Blandings went as well as expected. I used the pay telephone in the employee lounge to call the bandleader and explain I wouldn't able to sing with his combo for the time being, and that I was sorry. Part of me felt guilty for leaving the band in the lurch, and I hoped I hadn't burned a bridge. I made sure he knew I'd be happy to sing with them again, at someplace other than the Villa Italiana. On the other hand, plenty of aspiring singers were more than willing to take my place on stage. It wouldn't be hard to replace me. My regret was strong, but my resolve was stronger. If I wanted something different for myself, I'd have to make it happen. I only needed to figure out what. And how.

With that chore finished, Marjorie and I walked the several blocks to Union Station. As the train rolled out of Chicago, past the suburbs and small towns into open fields, the tension in my shoulders relaxed. I sank back in my seat. Mindful of Marjorie's warning that life in Kerryville could be duller than dust, I'd tucked two new novels in my bag: a Lord Peter Wimsey and the latest Agatha Christie. A whole weekend with little to do but read sounded luxurious-practically decadent.

When we stepped off at the Kerryville depot, the air smelled pure and fresh after the smog of the city. A tall, slim man with sand-colored hair approached us with a wide smile. Marjorie squealed and flung herself at him. I assumed this handsome specimen to be her fiancé, Richard Brownlee, until he released her and said, "Hey, sis. Don't you look swell. New duds?"

"You like?" Marjorie smiled and patted her new yellow cloche. Her obvious pleasure made me glow inside. I'd chosen the hat for her. I knew she'd love the new look, if she gave it a chance. Just like I knew she'd love wearing shorter skirts and bobbed hair and brightening her lips with High Society Red. Thanks largely to my advice, Marjorie finally looked as if she'd joined the twentieth century, even if she otherwise clung to convention.

She stepped back to include me in the circle.

"Let me introduce my brother, Charlie. Charlie, meet my roommate, Miss Dorothy Rodgers."

When he turned to me, I tried not to stare. But then, he was staring at me. Never had I seen such brilliant blue eyes-like Marjorie's, but bluer, if that were possible.

"Please call me Dot." I extended my hand and he took it in a strong grip. For one absurd moment I regretted wearing gloves, wondering what the skin of his hand would feel like against mine.

"Hello." Charlie grinned and shook my hand, then kept on grinning and shaking until I gently withdrew it.

"Charlie? Where's the car?" Marjorie piped up, breaking the spell.

He staggered back. "Oh. Uh, Betty's waiting over here." He hoisted my satchel and turned toward the street. Marjorie sighed, shook her head, and hoisted her own suitcase. Annoyed at her brother's lack of gallantry, I reached over to help her.

"It's all right. I can manage." Her smiling gaze met mine. "I pack lighter than you do."

As we followed Charlie, I noticed he walked with a distinct limp. And his arm–the one not holding my satchel–hung at an odd angle. I remembered Marjorie mentioning he'd served in France. A war hero. My heart melted a little in my chest. He didn't lack gallantry; he lacked a second strong arm.

"Who's Betty?" I stage-whispered to Marjorie, an unexpected feather of jealousy tickling the edge of my mind.

She smirked. "You'll see."

Betty turned out to be an old black Model T that, while showing her age, looked to be well kept. Unlike the men I knew who drove flashy cars in an effort to show off, Charlie's obvious affection for the humble vehicle impressed me far more.

On the short ride to the Corrigan home, I took in the scenery as Marjorie peppered her brother with questions about people and places I didn't know. The tree-lined streets, rambling

Victorian houses, and neat green lawns of Kerryville reminded me of Indiana. With any luck, the Corrigans would be a more pleasant family to spend time with than my own.

Charlie parked the Ford in front of a large white house with green trim. A tall, skinny girl shouted, "They're here," as she bounced off the porch and raced across the lawn, blond braids flying. She ran full-tilt into Marjorie, practically knocking her down.

"You must be Helen," I said, extending my hand. From Marjorie's description, I knew she was fifteen and full of pep.

The girl linked arms with her sister and me and hustled us toward the house.

A middle-aged woman with upswept iron-gray hair met us on the porch–Marjorie's stepmother, Frances. Though polite, the woman's smile did not quite reach her eyes as she shook my hand. When her gaze landed on Marjorie, she gasped. Apparently bobbed hair was not a hit with everyone.

"Golly, Frances," Helen broke in. "Doesn't she look like a movie star?"

"Don't say 'golly,' Helen. It's vulgar." Frances pressed her lips together as if to avoid saying anything further.

"How do you do, Mrs. Corrigan," I jumped in. "I've been so looking forward to meeting you."

"And I you," the older woman replied, but her voice lacked conviction.

"If you ladies will excuse me, I need to be getting back to the store." Charlie sidestepped the bags on the floor to pump my hand again. "Dinner's at seven, right, sis?"

"Right. The four of us, with Richard." Marjorie's face held an amused smile, as if she found her brother's enthusiasm entertaining. Me, I found it flattering.

We took our suitcases up to her room, freshened up, then returned to the porch, where Frances had set out cookies and lemonade. She seemed a little friendlier now. Maybe she'd recovered from her initial shock over two short-haired, short-skirted flappers standing on her porch in broad daylight for the whole neighborhood to see.

That evening, Charlie drove us to Kerryville's sole restaurant, the Tick-Tock Café. Before we went inside, he pointed out the green-and-white awning that marked Corrigan's Dry Goods, further down Main Street. I made suitable noises of admiration.

Marjorie's beau Richard met us in the foyer. One time Marjorie had shown me a photograph of him, in which he looked stiff and pompous. This impression was not dispelled in person, although he was rather good-looking in a quiet way: wavy light-brown hair, tall with an athletic build, and spectacles that made him look distinguished and wise. I supposed I could see what had attracted Marjorie to him, but why she stayed was a mystery, especially since I happened to know there was a much more interesting man vying for her attention back in Chicago. But that's another story, and hers to tell, not mine.

As we were shown to our table, I glanced around, taking in the ruffled gingham curtains and white-painted wooden tables, so vastly unlike any city nightspot with which I was familiar.

"Oh, isn't this just adorable?" I squealed in genuine delight. "I love small-town restaurants. So quaint."

Charlie looked deflated. "Kerryville must seem pretty unsophisticated compared to what you're used to in the big city."

I hastened to reassure him. "Kerryville's the Big Apple compared to where I came from."

"Which is ... ?"

"A tiny burg in Indiana. nothing more than a crossroads, really." I picked up the menu. "So, Charlie. You must bring dates here all the time. What do you recommend?"

He puffed up a little. "I rather like the steak, myself."

Across the table from us, Marjorie and Richard acted rather subdued for lovers who'd been apart for weeks. Hoping to liven the conversation, I ventured, "I can't wait to hear all about your work at the hospital, Dr. Brownlee. It must be terribly fascinating."

Richard's expression didn't change. "I don't know about fascinating, but I find it rewarding." He scanned the menu as if choosing his entrée was of the utmost importance. I bit back the temptation to recommend the cold fish.

Over dinner, having failed to get any useful conversation out of Richard, I beamed my full attention on Marjorie's brother. "Tell me all about what you do, Charlie."

And he did. With gusto. When Marjorie and Richard left the table to dance, we stayed seated. He told me all about Corrigan's Dry Goods and his plans for the store, how he'd someday like to expand it into a whole chain of stores. He quoted statistics from a retail-industry journal about successful chain stores like Piggly Wiggly and Ben Franklin. He could have been reading the dictionary, for all I cared. Because it wasn't his skills with managing inventory or arranging the stockroom that mattered. It was the man himself: a sweet, caring, kind man with a sincere heart. Sort of like a masculine form of Marjorie, come to think of it, with the trademark Corrigan optimism that let nothing hold them down. He was clearly a man of strong convictions.

And a man of strong convictions, sadly, would never consider getting mixed up in a love affair with a girl who worked in a speakeasy and dated men of questionable repute. I may not have been the brightest bulb in the chandelier, but that much I knew.

I said as much to Marjorie that night as we got ready for bed. Maybe not in so many words. But when she remarked on how well Charlie and I seemed to get along, I shrugged it off. No sense sending my heart where reality could never follow.

On Saturday afternoon, Marjorie and her stepmother labored at wedding tasks like compiling the guest list and working out the wording on the invitations. To my delight,

Charlie left work early and took me to a movie at the Orpheum. We watched some fluffy domestic comedy about mistaken identities resulting in mayhem and misunderstandings, with a suitably romantic conclusion.

Afterward we went to a place called Riley's for ice cream. With its massive oak bar, mirrored wall, dim interior, and scarred wooden tables, it had clearly been a tavern before Prohibition. Now that the sale of liquor had been outlawed, the place served banana splits instead of booze. Given my familiarity with such places, I felt more at home at Riley's than just about any other place in Kerryville–a fact I chose not to share with Charlie, as it was nothing to be proud of.

"How'd you like the picture?" I asked, dipping a spoon into the gooey chocolate syrup on my sundae.

"I liked it fine." He dug into a towering extravagance of vanilla and butterscotch, nuts and a cherry. "I was glad when the fellow ended up with the right girl."

I tilted my head. "Even though it meant giving up the beautiful starlet in favor of the plain Jane?"

He turned those crystal-blue eyes on me. "Sure. That's what every man wants, really, deep down. The simple things. A warm fire, a hearty meal, a good woman by his side."

I looked down at my sundae. *That's not what Louie wants,* I thought. *He'll go for the starlet, every time.*

"What about you ladies?" Charlie pressed. "What do you women want, more than anything?"

I lifted my spoon. "Chocolate and more chocolate."

He laughed, as I'd meant him to. But his question unsettled me. Before this weekend, I would have said I wanted thrills. Excitement. Freedom to do as I pleased. But in this moment, those words seemed empty. The peaceful, homespun picture he painted sounded infinitely more appealing.

He set down his spoon and leaned back in his chair. "Tell me about your family in Indiana."

I shrugged. "There's not much to tell. Mother, father, two younger sisters. I couldn't wait to get out of there."

He raised an eyebrow. "That rough?"

I sighed. "My father—my father's a difficult man." A shyster. A wolf who lies and steals money from innocent people, wrapped in the sheep's wool of an evangelist, a man of the cloth. I had no words to explain all that to this upstanding man, whom I'd likely never see again anyway. So I took a shortcut. "I guess you could say he and I didn't get along."

"I'm sorry to hear that." He paused. I was grateful he didn't pry. Then he said casually, "You know, I come into the city every so often. To meet with suppliers, that sort of thing." He glanced at me as if to gauge my reaction. "Maybe we could have dinner sometime."

My heart loved the idea, but my brain fired up a warning flare. "I don't know, Charlie," I said slowly. "Much as I'd like to, I'm awfully busy these days."

"I see." His voice chilled, and I felt sorry. There was nothing I'd have liked better than a date with Charlie Corrigan. But I saw no point in it. The better he got to know me, the more he'd discover the kind of girl I was and the sort of people I came from. Soon he'd hightail it back to Kerryville, where all the women were like Marjorie, singing in church choirs instead of speakeasies and dating doctors instead of bootleggers. Who needed that kind of heartache?

"Well, maybe I can write to you?" he said with a little less confidence. "You–you're not like any other woman I've ever met. I'd like to get to know you better."

I sighed. That's what I was afraid of. But despite my misgivings I heard my voice say, "Sure." No harm in having a pen pal. I didn't think he'd actually follow through, anyway. Most men of my acquaintance were lousy letter-writers.

We finished up our desserts and strolled back to the house. The easy banter between us had palled, and neither of us had much to say. I was careful not to take his arm or do anything that might be considered flirting. When we reached the house, Marjorie was sitting on the porch. I took a seat next to her, while Charlie settled on the wicker chair opposite.

"How was the movie?" she asked.

"It was all right," Charlie said. I could feel his gaze on my face, but I chose to examine a pot of geraniums instead of looking back, afraid of what I might see in his eyes. "Not much of a plot."

We made idle chitchat a while longer, then Charlie stood.

"Guess I'll go in and listen to the news with Pop."

I stood too. "I'm going to freshen up." What I really wanted was a cigarette, and some time alone to clear my head. I'd hurt Charlie's feelings, and that was the last thing I wanted to do.

I wound up standing alone in the backyard, leaning against a picnic table, cigarette in hand, trying to make sense of my feelings. I didn't belong here in Kerryville, among all these clean and decent people. So why was my attraction to Charlie so strong?

Marjorie came out the back door. "There you are." She sat next to me at the picnic table. I dropped the cigarette in the grass and crushed it with my shoe.

"Everything all right?" she asked
"Sure."

"Did something happen at the movies? You've been quiet since you got back."

I crossed my arms. "It's nothing. Charlie said some things that made me think. That's all." How could sweet Marjorie possibly understand what life was like for a girl like me?

Later, after Frances served a delicious caramel cake, Marjorie and I joined Pop in the living room, where he was reading the Chicago evening paper. I marveled aloud that the Daily News made it all the way to Kerryville.

"Can't rely on the Kerryville Bugle for anything beyond local sports scores and bridge-tournament results," Pop said genially, waving his pipe. "If it weren't for the Chicago papers and the radio, we'd never know what was going on in the world."

I picked up a section he'd left lying on the end table. "May I?"

"Help yourself."

If I wasn't going to spend my evenings with Louie anymore, I needed to find something else to do with my time. My eyes scanned the entertainment pages: movie reviews, book reviews, concert notices, a circus coming to town, and–

"Oh, my word," I uttered before I could stop myself. There on the page was a big, bold photograph of my father, along with an announcement that Oliver Barker, Evangelist, would soon be holding services at the Chicago Coliseum. Come one, come all.

"What is it?" Marjorie craned her neck to peer over my shoulder.

"It's–oh, it's nothing. Just something silly." I folded the paper, set it aside, and went to the kitchen on the pretense of helping with the washing up.

What could I have said? "Oh, I see here that my father, the famous and fraudulent evangelist, will be coming to town to fleece more people. Perhaps I can introduce you."

They'd put me on the first train back to Chicago. Alone.

♪

When Marjorie and I arrived back in Chicago the next day, a bouquet of roses waited on the coffee table in our apartment. For one fleeting moment, I hoped that Charlie'd sent them–an absurd thought. We'd only said good-bye at the station a few hours earlier, with vague promises to keep in touch. The idea that he'd immediately gallop over to a flower shop to order a bouquet was preposterous. Sure enough, the card was inked with Louie's name.

"Good golly," Marjorie breathed in wonder.

"What? They're just roses."

She pointed. I gasped.

There was not just one bouquet. Mounds of flowers, overflowing from boxes, abounding in vases, lay heaped on our little kitchen table.

"He just kept bringing 'em and bringing 'em," said the wide-eyed landlady, Mrs. Moran, who'd followed us upstairs from her apartment below ours. "Just kept bringing 'em and . . . "

"Yes, I see." I cut her off, embarrassed.

"Left telephone messages for you, too," Mrs. Moran continued, pulling a stack of loose papers from the pocket of her apron. "Lots of 'em. Got so bad, I finally turned off the ringer."

Heat rushed to my face as I took the handful of scrawled messages from her. "I'm so sorry for your trouble."

The kindly woman shook her gray head. "Not your fault, dearie. Clearly the man is smitten out of his mind."

No, he's not, I thought bitterly. *He just wants to think he can control me with his flowers and flattery. Well, not this time.* But outwardly I only smiled and thanked her, urging her to take an armload of flowers down to her apartment, which she did. When she was gone, Marjorie and I looked at each other.

"What are you going to do?" she whispered.

"Beats me," I said. "But what I'm not going to do is let him think that sending a few flowers will lure me back to the Villa Italiana, or to him."

After inviting Marjorie to choose the bouquet she liked best for her room, I stuffed the rest into the garbage can in the alley.

Charlie's first letter arrived on Tuesday, saying how much he'd enjoyed meeting me and expressing hope that business would soon bring him to Chicago. I crafted a careful reply to sound light and breezy and filled with news of the city, but no overtones of attraction or encouragement to visit. *Pen pals,* I reminded myself. Nothing more. *More* might mean he'd learn all about my past, and I couldn't let that happen.

Louie continued to call, and I continued to ignore his messages. One day while I was selling hats at Field's, he showed up at the store, something he'd never done before.

"Come on, Dottie," he pleaded, standing next to a display of berets, his hands spread in a beseeching gesture. "Didn't you get my flowers? My messages?"

"Stop it. Go away," I hissed, keeping an eye out for Mrs. Blandings, who didn't cotton to personal visitors during working hours.

"But the Villa Italiana needs you," he insisted. "I need you."

"You mean you haven't found a replacement singer."

He looked chagrined. "Nobody could replace you, Dottie."

I rolled my eyes.

His shoulders, under his snappy pinstripe suit jacket, slumped a little. "I admit it. I messed up real bad."

"Yes, you did."

His dark eyes were serious. "Look, Dottie. I know I don't deserve you. But the club absolutely does. Patrons have been asking about you, and the band hasn't been able to find a suitable replacement. Please come back and sing again. I'm begging you."

So there it was. It wasn't me he wanted. It was my vocal cords. Still, I felt my resolve weaken a crack. I did so love to sing, especially with the band. And frankly, I could've used the money. My hat-selling commissions only stretched so far.

But for whatever reason, something held me back from saying yes. Some unseen force–or maybe it was just the echo of Marjorie's voice saying, *You don't need him, Dot. You're worth more than that.*

My spine stiffened under my navy silk chemise.

"No. I'm sorry, Louie, the answer is no."

He stared at me, unaccustomed to that word falling from my lips where he was concerned. His dark eyes glittered. A muscle worked in his jaw.

"I'm warning you, Dottie. I won't ask again."

I swallowed hard. "Guess that's a chance I'll have to take."

♬

As summer faded into fall, Charlie and I kept up a steady stream of letters. He wrote wonderful letters filled with amusing observations of Kerryville life, and continued to hint at coming to the city. I wrote back, telling him about the store and other goings-on, but I didn't encourage him to visit. The farther he stayed away, the less he would know about me, and the easier it would be to get over my silly crush on him. He was my roommate's brother and we were becoming good friends, that's all. Or so I told myself.

"You shouldn't be alone in the evenings," Marjorie pronounced one morning, vigorously scraping the butter knife over her toast. "Louie might come over and pester you."

"He won't try anything," I said. "It wasn't me he wanted, anyway. He just wanted my pipes. I'm sure the band has found a replacement by now."

"Well, in any case, helping us get ready for the settlement house Christmas pageant will fill up your time."

The settlement house children's choir, a remarkable flock of ragtag children with angelic voices, had won over the crowd at the city's Fourth of July celebration in Grant Park. Now they'd been invited to participate in a Christmas pageant at the stately Orchestra Hall.

"As if my time needs filling," I muttered over my coffee cup, though I knew the truth. Without Louie and the Villa Italiana filling up my evenings, and with darkness falling earlier, I often felt lonely when Marjorie was out. Volunteering at the settlement house was her way of healing her heart, now that she'd finally broken off her engagement with Dr. Dull, but I couldn't imagine what it would do for mine.

"And you'll love getting to know all the people who work there," Marjorie insisted. "I know you will."

This I doubted very much. I'd known plenty of do-gooder types back in Indiana, in the church where my father preached when he wasn't on the road with his big pseudo-evangelistic circus. In my experience, do-gooders felt the same way he did about women who bobbed their hair and wore bright lipstick. And the more famous Father grew as a traveling evangelist, the more outspoken he became about denouncing such wickedness from the pulpit, all the while leading a private life that was nothing like the face he showed to the public. Under the guise of performing healing miracles, he took people's money with one hand and spent it on liquor and fast women with the other.

Which was why, when I received one particular letter from Charlie, I nearly hit the roof.

I may be coming to Chicago soon, he wrote. *I saw a notice in the paper that the famous evangelist Oliver Barker, following his successful tour last summer, is returning to offer a healing service at the Coliseum. I want to see if he can do something about these old war injuries of mine. The docs haven't been able to help me, and I'm sick and tired of limping around like an old man. I want to be able to take you dancing!*

Horrified, I grabbed my writing paper and fired off a blistering response.

Do NOT go to see Oliver Barker, I scrawled. *He's a sham and a fraud. I'm sure of this.* I bit the end of the pen, debating with myself how much to tell him. I thought I ought to come clean with the bald fact that Oliver Barker was my father. On the other hand, I was afraid that if I did, I would never see nor hear from Charlie Corrigan again. In the end, I chickened out. *I know someone who's intimately acquainted with him. I'm telling you, steer clear.*

Charlie's next letter carried no more nonsense about Oliver Barker. I breathed a sigh of relief. Through letters and phone calls, our friendship continued to grow, gradually blossoming into something deeper, in spite of my supposed determination to the contrary.

At the same time, strange yearnings stirred in me. I found myself wanting to become more like Marjorie. When we'd first met, I thought she was the sorriest thing I'd ever laid eyes on, with her frumpy sweaters and mousy demeanor. But as I got to know her, I gradually realized that what I saw as mousiness was really a kind and gentle spirit. Her supposed frumpiness was a sort of feminine modesty with which I was unfamiliar. Her beauty glowed quietly, like a candle. Next to her I felt like a blinking neon sign, and just as cheap. I wanted what she had, to figure out what made her tick.

That curiosity, on top of the crushing boredom of being stuck at home alone in the evenings, found me stepping off the streetcar with her one chilly autumn evening. Directly across the street stood the settlement house, a former mansion turned neighborhood center for the immigrant community surrounding it. Apprehension weighted my chest, but to my surprise, I was warmly welcomed by everyone there. No one seemed to care who I was or where I came from, what I'd done, or who my father was. Other than Marjorie, I knew only one of the other volunteers: Ruthie, who worked in the stationery department at Field's. The other volunteer on duty that evening, a dark-haired woman named Annamarie, smiled warmly as we were introduced.

"Marjorie tells me you like to sing," she said. "How would you like to run the children's choir through their paces?"

I gulped. Apart from my two younger sisters back in Indiana, I wasn't used to dealing with children.

"I don't know . . . I thought maybe I could work on costumes or something."

Sensing my hesitation, Annamarie said, "It would be such a great help if you would work with their singing. They have natural talent but it needs to be developed. I've got lots of more pressing tasks to take care of, Ruthie's busy running the games, and Marjorie here–"

"–can't carry a tune in a bucket," my roommate broke in. "Please, Dot. The concert's only a few weeks away. You're the perfect one to lead the singing."

I was introduced to the children as "Miss Dot." At first, they struck me as a chaotic bunch of screaming hair-pullers, rubber-ball-bouncers, and paper-airplane-flingers. But once I got the hang of corralling them and seizing their attention, I found I enjoyed getting them to sing.

"You take a deep breath way, way down in your belly, like this." I put a hand on my midsection and inhaled, then sang like a mezzo soprano at the opera, "This way your voice is supported and you can hold your notes longerrr." I rolled my r's like Rosa Ponselle.

The children laughed. With the ice broken, we went on to have a good rehearsal, and several more after that. Annamarie opened every rehearsal with a prayer. The first few times, I just bowed my head. But gradually I found myself praying along. After all, what could it hurt?

I encouraged two especially talented high-school girls, Gabriella and Bianca, to sing a duet in the concert, and spent extra time coaching them. Between the Christmas rush at Field's and rehearsals every night, I became so busy, I practically forgot about Louie and the club. I didn't even miss singing on stage. Helping the children sing was a new way to participate in music, and gave me surprising satisfaction.

Louie stopped bothering me, but not out of any sense of nobility on his part. One eventful evening, the Villa Italiana was raided. In spite of Louie's chummy arrangements with various members of the Chicago police force, the Feds caught up with him, and he landed in jail. I can't say I missed him one bit.

But I did miss Charlie Corrigan.

Little by little, letter by letter, I let him into my heart. One quiet evening, he surprised me by showing up on our Chicago doorstep. Marjorie and I were both thrilled to see him, but my delight turned to dismay when he revealed the real reason for his visit over dinner at a Chinese restaurant.

"Now don't get steamed," he said. "I'm going to that revival meeting at the Coliseum tonight."

"Oh, Charlie. No. I told you. Reverend Barker is nothing but a big con man. Why, he has no more healing powers than a magical toad in a fairy tale. Don't be a fool."

"What are you two talking about?" Marjorie broke in. "Who's Reverend Barker?"

"He's a healer," Charlie said. "He's helped lots of others, and he can help me. I know he can. But Dot doesn't believe it."

I was furious. "Your brother thinks a traveling carnival man can perform healing miracles. Well, you can do as you like, Charlie Corrigan. But I want no part of it." I grabbed my purse and stormed out of the restaurant to hail a cab. But by the time the vehicle pulled up in front of the two-flat, my heart rate had slowed and I was thinking more clearly. I leaned forward.

"I changed my mind. Please take me to the Coliseum."

"Whatever you say, lady." The cabbie pressed the meter.

By the time the taxi pulled up in front of the hulking Coliseum, the service was well underway. I refused to go inside and stood in the shadows near the entrance instead. I didn't want to risk being spotted by my father or one of the people who worked for him. Such an encounter could only lead to trouble.

When Charlie eventually came out-every bit as lame as he'd gone in, of course-my heart cracked in two. Marjorie was with him, and she was saying something, touching his arm. I couldn't hear her words, but the expressions on their faces told me all I needed to know. Charlie looked up at my approach.

"You came," he said quietly.

"Yes. I've been here the whole time."

He looked at the ground. "You wasted your time. Nothing to see here."

My throat constricted. I eased my arms around his shoulders and pressed my forehead against his collar. He pulled me close. We both stood there for a long minute while people brushed past us.

"Charlie, I'm so sorry," I said over and over. He didn't say anything, just stood with his face buried in my hair. At last, he lifted his head.

"I wanted to be whole, Dot. I wanted to be a whole man–for you."

I pounded his shoulder with my fist. "You idiot. Don't you know I love you just the way you are?"

There. I'd said it out loud. And the world didn't come to a screeching halt in its orbit.

Apparently, he wasn't buying it, though.

"I should've listened to you."

I grasped his shoulders and looked squarely into his face. "Charlie, I'd give anything to be wrong. Anything. But he's nothing but a fake."

"But he seemed so convincing. How could you be so sure?"

I gave a derisive snort. "That's easy. Reverend Barker is my father."

♫

Over coffee in a diner later that evening, I spilled my guts to him and Marjorie. I told them what it was like growing up with a traveling faux-evangelist for a father, the night he wanted me to fake an illness and pretend to be "healed," the hurtful words he'd shouted when I refused, our acrimonious parting when I finally came of age. To my amazement, none of it seemed to bother either of them in the least. Instead, they were sympathetic.

"Well, your father may be a fraud," Marjorie said, "but not all Christians are."

"I think I know that now," I said. "I'm beginning to anyway, thanks to you two."

"Know what I think?" Charlie stirred a spoonful of sugar into his coffee. "I think you ought to go and see him," Charlie said.

"What?"

"Talk to him. Try to reconcile your relationship."

"Are you crazy?" I sighed. "Have you heard a word I've said?"

"There's a lot he's done wrong," Charlie said. "But refusing to forgive him is eating you up inside. And it's confounding your understanding of God."

I didn't want to acknowledge it then, but the truth of his words hit home not long afterward, when Pop Corrigan suffered a heart attack. Although Pop pulled through, Charlie had little time to spend in Chicago–and I had a whole lot of time to think about God and family and what it all meant. I didn't come to any firm conclusions, but I gave it plenty of thought.

Later, after we dropped Marjorie off at the apartment, Charlie and I drove to the lakeshore and sat in the car, watching moonlight dance off the dark water. The night air was tinged with frost, but in the warmth of each others' arms, we felt none of the cold. By the time he took me home, the last of my doubts about the depth of his feelings had drifted away on the waves.

♫

On the afternoon of the settlement-house Christmas show, I was practically out the door when Mrs. Moran stopped me in the vestibule.

"Dot, you're wanted on the telephone."

"Is it Louie? Because if it is, please tell him-"

The landlady interrupted me. "No, it's a woman's voice."

Sighing, I entered her apartment, sat at the little telephone table in the corner, and picked up the earpiece.

"Hello?"

"Dot? It's Annamarie, from the settlement house."

The urgent tone in her voice made me sit up straighter.

"Annamarie? I was just leaving to go over to the auditorium for dress rehearsal."

"Bianca's mother sent word that Bianca has a sore throat and a high fever. They've called for the doctor. She won't be able to perform tonight."

I slumped. "Oh, no. Poor thing. Well, how do you think Gabriella would feel about doing the number solo?"

"That's the thing," Annamarie said. "Gabriella's petrified at the thought of going on stage alone. Besides, the part she's memorized is mostly harmony. She'd have to learn an entirely new part by tonight. Bianca carried most of the melody."

"I see." I twisted the telephone cord around my finger. "But that number is one of the highlights. It would leave a terrible gap in the program to cut it. We were relying on that song to give other singers time for a costume change."

"That's why I'm calling you. Gabriella wants to know if you'll sing Bianca's part."

"Me?" A rock landed in the pit of my stomach. "I haven't sung for an audience since . . . " Since the speakeasy. "Well, in quite a while."

"But you've been working on it with the girls for weeks. You know it by heart."

"That's true, bu–" I thought for a moment longer, then said, "All right. Tell Gabriella I'll take Bianca's part."

"Oh, thank you. She'll be so relieved." Annamarie's voice audibly brightened.

I thanked Mrs. Moran for the use of the telephone, then trotted back upstairs to my apartment and into my bedroom. I flung open the closet door and started rooting around. I needed something to wear that was both elegant and modest–not a sparkly, spangly, speakeasy gown. At last I uncovered a forgotten dress, ivory silk draped in layers, like something a noblewoman in ancient Greece would wear. I'd worn it once at the Villa Italiana, and Louie had declared it too sedate. Which meant that it was probably ideal for the stage at Orchestra Hall.

Hastily I packed the dress and a few accessories and cosmetics into a satchel and ran back downstairs. At the streetcar stop, I hailed a taxi. There was no time to waste. Gabriella and I would need as much practice as we could get before showtime.

As giddy children took their places, I paced nervously backstage. I hadn't had time to tell anyone I'd be singing, but Marjorie appeared, carrying a dress she'd made for Gabriella. The young girl couldn't have been more ecstatic. While she was off changing her clothes, I quickly filled Marjorie in on what had happened.

"I'll let Charlie know you won't be sitting with us," she said. Then a smile crept up her face. "On second thought, I think I'll let it be a surprise to see you up there."

"I don't know. It makes me awful nervous to sing, knowing he's out there," I admitted. "But this is a whole new kind of song–one that I think he'll like."

We shared a laugh, which broke the tension and made me feel better about the whole situation. A new song, for a new kind of girl. As Marjorie gave me a quick hug and returned to her seat in the audience, I no longer felt nervous, just excited.

At last Gabriella and I stepped out onto the stage. The orchestra floated the opening notes. We took a collective breath and began.

*While shepherds watched their flocks by
night,*
all seated on the ground,
the angels of the Lord sang 'round
and glory shone around,
and glory shone around.

I felt Gabriella slip her hand into mine as we paused between verses. I squeezed and she squeezed back. Inside I felt all warm and glowing. Was this a small taste of what Marjorie had that I didn't? Of what Charlie had?

"Fear not," said he for mighty dread
Had seized their troubled minds.
"Glad tidings of great joy I bring
To you and all mankind,
To you and all mankind."

The glare of the spotlight turned most of the audience into mere shadows, but I thought I could pick out the Corrigan family. There was Marjorie and Frances and Helen and–and, yes, Pop was there, too. Thank goodness, he felt well enough to come. And Charlie. Dear, dear Charlie.

The orchestra swelled on the introduction to the third verse, and my heart swelled with it.

Thus spake the seraph, and forthwith
Appeared a shining throng
Of angels praising God, who thus
Addressed their joyful song,
Addressed their joyful song.

All glory be to God on high
And on the earth be peace;
Goodwill henceforth from heav'n to men
Begin and never cease,
Begin and never cease.

The unlikelihood of a former speakeasy singer standing center-stage at Orchestra Hall, singing her heart out to God, was not lost on me. All those words about Jesus' birth and joy and peace settled in my heart. I came to a decision. I wanted that joy and peace for myself. I wasn't sure how, but I knew that Marjorie and Charlie and Annamarie and so many others would point me in the right direction.

After the concert, everyone gathered in the lobby over coffee and cookies, basking in the afterglow and congratulating the choir, Gabriella and me in particular, on the performance. I thanked them, but I knew it wasn't our doing. Something extraordinary had happened up there.

As we were collecting our wraps from the coat check, Helen said, "I know. Let's all go see Marjorie's windows!"

Laughing and huddling close for warmth, we all traipsed over to State Street, then the couple blocks north to Field's, easing our way into the milling crowd of package-laden shoppers gathered in front of the huge plate-glass windows. Over the course of the fall, Marjorie had left Ladies' Nightwear and been hired as a window trimmer under the direction of the famous Arthur Fraser–her dream job. She and the rest of Mr. Fraser's team had indeed outdone themselves, creating an enchanting spectacle of gently falling snow, mannequins resplendent in velvet and taffeta, and piles of shiny wrapped packages stashed under a larger-than-life Christmas tree. As the family oohed and aahed, Charlie pulled me aside.

"You really did sound divine," he said. "Even now, you look . . . I don't know. Different. Like some of that stardust got in your eyes."

I smiled. "I've been mulling over what you said. About the importance of family and . . . and everything. And I've made a decision. I think I should go home to Indiana for Christmas. See if I can get my father to listen to me."

"You are?" His blue eyes sparkled. "That's wonderful."

I nodded. "If I've learned anything from your father's heart attack, it's that family is important. I'd hate to live my whole life without–well, you know. Without trying to make things right."

"Yes, I know." He slipped his arms around me and pulled me close. "For what it's worth, I think you're doing the right thing."

I raised my head and placed my cheek against his. The bracing chill of his skin against mine comforted me and gave me courage.

I turned my face just enough for his lips to find mine. I kissed him with all the love in my heart, no longer feeling the cold. The whole world faded while I embraced the man I loved.

The voices of his family forced us to break the kiss, but he didn't release me from his arms. "I'll be praying that all goes well with your family, especially your father," he murmured. "But I'll miss you very much."

"It's terrible to be apart on Christmas," I admitted. "But I'll be back before New Year's Eve."

He released me and grinned. "Then we'll spend New Year's Eve together here in Chicago. It's a date. And maybe this year will be the last Christmas ever that we'll spend apart."

My throat tightened. "Oh, wouldn't that be the cat's pajamas," I breathed. I slipped my arm through his as we trailed the others down the sidewalk.

"Come on, you two slowpokes," Helen called, her breath frosty on the air. "Come join the rest of the family."

We laughed and quickened our pace. My heart felt as if it might burst out of my chest.

Family.

I liked the sound of that.

The Christmas Robe

Say the word "Christmastime" and most people think of manger scenes and jingle bells, the glow of colored lights and the flutter of angels' wings. But at the great Marshall Field & Company, Chicago's premier department store, Christmastime meant all that and more, along with enough crowds, clanging, and clatter to shatter a sales clerk's nerves. I know this because that clerk was me.

I can't remember now what the problem was, that early December afternoon back in the '20s—some shortcoming involving a woolen bed jacket, I believe. As the customer ranted, my brain fogged over. My only thought was that her flushed face made nearly a precise match to the holly berries nestled in the evergreen garland festooning the shelf right behind her head. Normally our supervisor, Mrs. Cross, would step in and smooth things over—no customer would leave her section dissatisfied!—but Ladies'

Nightwear was as hectic as Union Station at rush hour and she was directing traffic over by the emerald silk hostess gowns, clear on the other side of the department.

When the customer had finally stormed off and I had a moment to catch my breath, Mrs. Cross scurried over and blessed me with the assignment of unpacking a fresh shipment of garments in the stockroom. Usually we clerks balked at the banishment of stockroom duty, which meant fewer dollars penciled neatly into our sales ledgers, but this time I leaped at the chance to escape the madness of the sales floor. Between my aching back and burning feet and the hordes of frenzied shoppers eager to commemorate the birth of our Lord with flannel pajamas and satin housecoats, I was desperate for a few moments of peace.

"Hurry, Miss Corrigan," Mrs. Cross urged in an exaggerated stage-whisper. "It's the Queen Maries."

I quickened my step. According to the buyer for Ladies' Nightwear, the Queen Marie boudoir robe was to be the star in our crown, the centerpiece of our holiday sales strategy, but they'd been delayed at the manufacturer. Getting the darn things steamed, priced, and out onto the sales floor was a matter of utmost urgency, if Ladies' Nightwear was to make a good showing in the December sales figures next to all the other sections of the store.

"Be sure to tell customers that it's an exact copy of a style owned by Queen Marie. An exact copy." The buyer for Ladies' Nightwear had been breathless in her enthusiasm as she described the robe to the sales staff. I'd rolled my eyes–how exciting could a bathrobe be?–but with the royal moniker attached, it was sure to be an easy sale. Earlier that fall, Queen Marie of Romania had visited Chicago as part of a nationwide tour, and had even stopped at Field's. Her visit had caused a publicity sensation, and women across the city were still giddy with Queen Marie fever.

Perched on a stepstool in the claustrophobic stockroom, I knew the moment I sliced open the carton that this was no ordinary robe. Fashioned of deep crimson silk velvet, with creamy Belgian lace at the collar and cuffs and the most exquisite tailoring along the yoke, it was flawless.

With care bordering on reverence I lifted the top robe and hugged it to myself. The lace tickled my nose, and the heavy velvet lay smooth and rich in my hands. As I breathed in the scent of luxury, daydreams flickered across my imagination like a Mary Pickford movie. With my wedding coming up, I'd been keeping an eye out for a new robe to add to my trousseau. My mind spooled out a vision of the perfect morning when I'd serve my new husband the fluffiest of pancakes, and hot coffee in a delicate china cup, while swathed head-to-toe in crimson velvet. With admiration shining in his eyes, he'd lift his crystal goblet of freshly squeezed orange juice and say how very lucky he was to have chosen me as his bride. Of course, I didn't own any china cups, not to mention crystal goblets, but that's what wedding presents were for, and anyway, the first step was–

"Marjorie, how are you coming with those robes?" Mrs. Cross poked her head around the stockroom curtain, her strident voice shattering my dream. She only used my first name when we were out of earshot of customers.

"Oh, um, fine," I said, and she retreated. Gently, I slid the first robe onto a hanger and hung it on a wheeled rack, then stood back and admired it full-length. My heart thumped at the beauty of it. I reached deeply into the carton and pulled out the inventory sheet to check the price.

I blinked.

Surely that figure wasn't right.

I blinked again.

It was.

Now my heart thumped for a different reason. I gave a low whistle. The Queen Marie was the most expensive garment Ladies' Nightwear had ever carried. With a sinking sensation I realized that, even with my employee discount, there would be no way I could ever afford to own such a robe. I sighed. Easy come, easy go. My Beloved would simply have to put up with the sight of me in a boring ordinary bathrobe, pouring his coffee into a ceramic mug. A chipped one, at that.

Swallowing my disappointment, I finished hanging all of the gorgeous garments on the rack and steamed them free of wrinkles. Then I grabbed a pen and a handful of blank tags from a nearby shelf. I filled out the price tags, pinned them to the inside cuffs of the robes, and wheeled the rack out onto the sales floor. Immediately a small band of ladies gathered around, oohing and aahing and brushing eager fingers over the fabric. With a heavy sigh, I turned away to help the next shopper clamoring for my attention.

♫

"My goodness. All this fuss about a bathrobe?" my roommate, Dot, remarked that evening.

"It's the most beautiful thing you've ever seen," I said, "like something Gloria Swanson would wear. I can just picture myself wearing it on our honeymoon." I described to her my breakfast daydream starring my beloved and his crystal goblet of orange juice.

"... as bluebirds and turtledoves sing outside the latticed window of your rose-covered cottage," Dot quipped with a not-so-subtle note of sarcasm. She peered intently at her fingernails as she painted them with cherry-red lacquer. "If you ask me, that's an awful lot of clams to shell out for a bathrobe."

I crossed my arms. "You have no sense of romance."

She blew a puff of air over her nails. "Look, Marjorie. I'm as romantic as the next girl, but I'm just being honest. I've watched you cook breakfast. You're likely to end up with pancake batter down the front of that gorgeous bathrobe, and toast crumbs in your hair."

"Boudoir robe," I muttered, ignoring the accuracy of her prediction.

"Look, doll, you're better off saving your money and buying a pretty new hat instead."

"You would say that," I scoffed. "You work in Millinery."

She shrugged. "Suit yourself. But a new cloche or beret would be admired by a lot more people than a bathrobe."

"Boudoi–oh, never mind." I heaved a sigh. "It doesn't matter anyway. There's no way I could ever afford it."

But hope came just a couple of weeks later, in the unlikely form of my fellow clerk, Miss Ryan. Much as the public seemed to adore the celestial robes, they didn't adore the celestial price. We'd only managed to sell a handful, in spite of the Christmas rush.

I remarked as much to Miss Ryan one afternoon during a rare lull in the action.

"They're going half-price the day after Christmas," she said. "I overheard the buyer saying so to Mrs. Cross."

I fought to remain calm. "Half price? Really?" It would still be an enormous stretch, but with my employee discount, and if we received a holiday bonus ...

"Sure is," Miss Ryan said, "and it's a terrible thing, too. Old Rugged is upset about it. She was counting on those robes making Ladies' Nightwear look good to the top brass."

"Oh. That is terrible," I agreed, trying to sound disappointed. But inside I rejoiced. All I had to do was hold out and buy the robe the day after Christmas, and all would be well. I was so confident in this plan that, in a sudden spurt of generosity, I donated my old blue terrycloth bathrobe to the church Christmas pageant, where it would clothe some shepherd abiding in the field, keeping watch over his flock by night. Meanwhile, while I was between robes, I'd throw an old cardigan over my nightgown and shiver.

But a few days later, disaster struck. Miss Kimbrough, a copywriter from the advertising office, strode through our section, clipboard in hand, hot on the trail of new merchandise to feature in a special sales advertisement. She and Mrs. Cross conversed *tête-à-tête*, and then I saw Old Rugged make a gesture toward the Queen Maries. My heart sank. Clearly she was recommending that Miss Kimbrough write about them! Miss Kimbrough had an ingenious way with words, and I knew that the minute she applied her special magic to the ad, the robes would fly out the door and there would be none left for me.

When their conversation ended, I waited until Mrs. Cross was out of earshot, then intercepted Miss Kimbrough and pointed out the rack of woolen bed jackets that (as it turned out) itched like the dickens. I tried to talk her into featuring those in her ad instead of the Queen Maries, to no avail. The Queen Marie boudoir robe was featured prominently in that Sunday's *Tribune*, and sure enough, wealthy matrons poured into Ladies' Nightwear to snap them up at full price. Just a few days before Christmas, there were almost none left. Mrs. Cross was ecstatic. I was panicking. I simply had to have one!

So I did the unthinkable. When no one was looking, I took the last remaining Queen Marie in my size, folded it up, and hid it under a tall stack of lounging slacks. Those slacks, by virtue being dyed an unearthly shade of puce, were such slow sellers, I didn't worry much that my ruse would be discovered.

Hoarding merchandise was strictly against store policy, of course. I could have lost my job for it, if I were caught. And when it came time to pay for the robe and take it home, I'd have to conjure up some excuse for why I still had a Queen Marie in my possession, if they'd supposedly sold out. But I'd cross that bridge when I came to it.

On Christmas Eve, Ladies' Nightwear was a madhouse until around 3 p.m. when, as if responding to some silent universal signal, the customers dwindled, heading home through the snow to their cozy firesides and cheerful family gatherings. We'd sold the last of the Queen Marie robes except, of course, for the one I'd secretly stashed away. I congratulated myself on my wisdom and foresight.

Wearied from the onslaught, but buoyed by the thought of the church Christmas pageant to come that evening, followed by a sound night's sleep and a Christmas morning that would surely include a diamond ring, I offered to begin sweeping up the debris of the day while Mrs. Cross and Miss Ryan took a well-deserved break. Behind me someone cleared his throat. I turned to see a young workingman, standing hat in hand, a merry sprig of holly tucked into the lapel of his worn coat. I straightened and smiled.

"Hello there. Merry Christmas."

"And a merry Christmas to you." He shifted his weight and turned his rough woolen cap over and over in his hands.

"What can I do for you?"

"I've come to buy a present for my wife." His face beamed and he stood a little taller. "I've come for that Queen Marie robe."

Squelching my surprise that a workingman would want such a luxurious garment, I said, "Oh, I'm terribly sorry. They're gone."

"Gone?" Puzzlement clouded his face, as if he didn't quite grasp the language.

"They've been sold," I said. "All of them. I'm so sorry. But I can suggest a lovely–"

"No," he blurted with startling conviction. "They can't be gone." He stared at the space where the robes had hung, now occupied by a rack of flannel nightgowns covered in a snowflake pattern, the harbinger of our January "Adorable Alpine" theme.

"W-well, yes, I'm afraid they are. But if you'll just step this way–"

"I can pay for it," he said. My heart cracked at the earnest look in his eyes. From the pocket of his work pants he pulled out fist after fist of coins and bills, laying them with a great clatter on the glass countertop. "I've been working overtime, see, saving every penny. I even sold my old baseball glove. Took a while to get the money, else I would have come sooner. But I can pay for it."

"I'm sure you can," I quickly assured him, placing a hand on his rough sleeve. "That's not the problem. The problem is, we have no more of them left. Zero. Zilch."

Except for the one hidden under a stack of puce lounging slacks.

No, I said to the Presence who suddenly flooded my conscience. *He can't have it. It's mine.*

The man's face spoke of desperation. "Will you be getting any more?"

I shook my head. "Not this year, no. But it did prove to be a very popular style, so if you come back next year, perhaps a little earlier, we may have it again, or something quite similar."

He looked straight at me, eyes glistening. "Next year will be too late." He wrung the cap in his hands. "She's ... she won't be here."

"Who won't be here?"

"My wife. She's ... you see, it's her lungs ..."

The blood rushed to my head as his meaning became clear. "Oh." For once I had no words.

"The doctors say six months, maybe." He spoke in a rush. "Our place is so drafty, and she fell head over heels for that robe, that day we come in here. She don't talk of nothing else, and I thought it might, you know, keep her plenty warm in this here world, before ..." His voice cracked. He swallowed hard, then began sweeping the pile of bills and coins into his large rough hands. "Well, never mind, miss. It ain't your fault." He glanced up. "Maybe I'll take one of them snowflake nightgowns instead," he said without enthusiasm. "That'll keep her warm enough, and I won't go home empty-handed."

I swallowed hard myself, trying to choke the words back, but they flowed out anyway.

"I just remembered something," I croaked. "Wait here." I slipped over to the puce lounging slacks, reached underneath the stack, and returned bearing a treasure, in all its crimson velvet glory.

The very last Queen Marie. My eyesight blurred as I laid it on the counter.

His eyes bulged in amazement. "You–you found one!"

"Yes." To my astonishment, the words kept flowing. "And I'll let you in on a little secret. It's going to be half-price day after tomorrow. But I'm going to sell it to you for half-price tonight." The words left my mouth before I could stop them. But for some reason, stopping them no longer seemed important.

The man's eyes widened. "Are you sure, miss?"

"I've never been surer of anything." And to my great surprise, it was the truth.

I wrote out the sales receipt for half-price, and took his money. Then I carefully wrapped the robe in tissue and slid it into a gift box, along with a hastily scribbled note. "If you take this to the gift-wrapping department, the girls will wrap it up in pretty paper. Show them this note, and it will be free of charge."

"Oh, thank you, miss," he breathed. "You're an angel."

"Believe me, I'm not," I insisted, ashamed at how close I'd come to hoarding it for myself.

He tipped his cap. "A very merry Christmas to you, miss."

"And to you. And tell your wife–tell her to have a very merry Christmas, too. God bless you."

"He already has."

A lump formed in my throat as I watched him walk away with the package under his arm, whistling. I sent up a silent prayer for him and his wife, that maybe God in His mercy would write a different ending to their story, after all.

Then I ripped up the sales receipt and wrote a fresh one for the full price of the robe. I attached the man's money to it, then pulled my pocketbook from the drawer, opened my wallet, counted out the remainder, and put it with the day's receipts to be turned in to the cashier at closing time.

As I continued sweeping, I thought of my old blue robe, which suddenly seemed magnificent. Because my Beloved liked blue, which he said brought out the color of my eyes. Because it was easily washed when sprinkled with spilled coffee and toast crumbs. Because it would be worn that night by a shepherd worshiping at a manger, and because the original manger had held a Baby who'd changed everything when He came to save the world. That's what Christmas was all about. Somehow, in the rush of customers and carolers and crimson velvet, I'd lost the whole point of the story.

Some other bride would be wrapped in velvet that Christmas. And that was all right by me. I already had everything needed to–as the young man put it so eloquently–keep me plenty warm in this here world.

Playing for Keeps

"Next stop, Rathdrum, Idaho."

At the conductor's bellow, I consulted the dog-eared Northern Pacific timetable clutched in my damp palm, then stared out the train's grimy window. After three days on the North Coast Limited, it hardly seemed possible I'd arrived at last. A shiver of delight coursed down my spine.

I peered into the little mirror glued inside the lid of my travel case. Hair combed, check. Face washed, check. My complexion looked pale, and faint shadows ringed my eyes, but there was nothing to be done about that. At fifteen I was too young to wear face powder. Or so decreed my stepmother, Frances.

An hour earlier I'd latched myself into the restroom and changed into a fresh dress–blue cotton with embroidered cuffs and a white rolled collar. I yearned to show my old friend, Maisie Summerfield, that I was no longer a dungaree-wearing tomboy, at least not all the time.

But a change of clothes did only so much good. Frankly, I needed a long, hot bath. Did the Summerfields even have a bathtub? Out in the untamed Idaho wilderness, a luxurious modern amenity like indoor plumbing might not be a given. I knew this thanks to my fondness for dime novels in which plucky spinsters headed West to escape overbearing relatives and found primitive living conditions–along with romance, if they were lucky, which they usually were.

In her letters, Maisie had gushed about thick forests, towering mountains, and sparkling lakes. While she never stated outright that her family lived in a rustic log cabin tucked away in the backcountry, I could read between the lines. I imagined her churning butter and chopping wood–an impression strengthened as the train chugged through the rugged Northern Rockies.

I stiffened my spine. If a hot bath was not to be had, I vowed to be gracious and uncomplaining. Hardships were to be expected as part of this great Idaho adventure. It would be fun, like last summer's trip to Camp Minne-WaWa, minus the poison ivy.

I snapped the case shut. I'd looked forward to this trip for weeks, ever since Frances had received a letter from Mrs. Summerfield inviting me to spend part of summer vacation with her daughter. Maisie had been my best chum at Kerryville Grammar School until three years ago, when her father's new job with a big lumber mill uprooted her family to Idaho. When our teacher pointed to Idaho on the schoolroom map, my heart sank at the vast distance between there and Illinois.

At last the engine steamed into the Rathdrum depot. I swiped at the smudged window with my hankie and thought of my last conversation with Maisie at the Kerryville station.

"You'll write to me?" Her eyes had looked suspiciously misty.

"Of course, silly. Every week."

I'd meant it, too. At first our letters had flown thick and fast. But then school and dramatics club and baseball practice had eaten up my time. Maisie was busy, too. Gradually our letters dwindled from weekly to once-in-a-while.

But that was all about to change. Now we'd pick up our friendship exactly where we'd left off. I reached into my pocket and fingered the gift I'd brought: a hefty, cobalt-blue cats-eye marble, a real beauty of a shooter. I'd coveted it for a long time, and finally won it fair and square from Sammy Wardlow while playing for keeps. Now I was giving it to Maisie, because if ever a girl was an ace at shooting marbles, it was her.

Anxiously I scanned the platform. Only a few people stood waiting: a man wearing a brown fedora pulled down over his eyes, another man in overalls, and two well-dressed ladies standing together. No sign of Maisie.

I peered again at the man in the fedora. Perhaps Maisie's father had been sent to fetch me. But this man didn't look like Mr. Summerfield, as best I could recall. I swallowed hard. What if everyone forgot I was coming?

My gaze slid back to the two ladies, and my heart lurched. It wasn't two ladies: it was Maisie and her mother. Maisie was practically grown-up!

I stood, grabbed my case, and followed the other passengers off the train.

"Hello!" I shouted, waving my arm.

Maisie whirled around. "Helen! There you are."

I dropped the case and flew at my friend, enveloping her in an ecstatic hug that knocked her hat askew. As we embraced, I noticed two things: how very tall Maisie had gotten, and how she was surrounded by the scent of roses. As for myself, I was certain I must stink to high heaven of soot and axle grease and worse.

"Let me look at you." Maisie held me at arm's length, eyes sparkling. "It's so lovely to see you."

"And how!" I returned the grin, but suddenly felt awkward. So lovely to see you? Since when did Maisie say things like so lovely to see you? That was grown-up talk. Who was this stranger?

We stood gawking at each other like goofs. Not only was my friend tall and rose-scented, but she wore lip rouge the color of ripe strawberries, and her formerly waist-length hair had been chopped short around her ears, topped by a fashionable cloche. My own lips were bare, and my locks hung in two childish braids down my back, bobbed hair and lip rouge being two more things that Frances didn't approve of.

Mrs. Summerfield kissed my cheek. "You must be exhausted after your trip, Helen, dear," she said in her gracious way.

Yes. Yes, that was it. I was tired. Everything would seem less strange after a good rest. And a bath, because it was clear from Maisie's appearance that the Summerfields did indeed own a bathtub.

After we'd collected my luggage, Mrs. Summerfield led the way toward a shiny silver roadster parked nearby.

I blinked. "Jeepers. This is yours?"

Maisie laughed and said, "Of course. What did you expect? A lumber truck?"

I echoed her laugh and adjusted my assumptions. I watched in admiration as Mrs. Summerfield slid behind the wheel. Not many women back in Kerryville drove their own automobiles.

We drove across a flat prairie ringed with mountains, then into the bustling town of Coeur d'Alene. My shyness faded as Maisie prattled on, asking questions about my trip and about people we both knew back home. I found it easier to talk to her if I kept my gaze on the scenery instead of on the poised and polished stranger sitting beside me.

Mrs. Summerfield pointed out the newly built Federal Building and Courthouse, as imposing and governmental-looking as anything back east. Sherman Avenue was lined on either side with intriguing-looking shops and cafes, even a movie theater. To my surprise, Coeur d'Alene didn't look much different from Kerryville, except for the mountains.

"Here we are," Mrs. Summerfield said at last, pulling into the driveway of a splendid white American foursquare with a wide, inviting porch and an emerald lawn that swept clear down to the sparkling waters of Lake Coeur d'Alene.

The last shred of my log-cabin vision whirled away on the lake breeze. Whatever Mr. Summerfield's job was over at that logging mill, he clearly didn't do it in sap-stained overalls.

Mrs. Summerfield gave me a quick tour of the spacious downstairs rooms, filled with sunlight and smelling of lemon oil and beeswax. Then she suggested I take a rest before dinner. Maisie helped me unpack in her sunny bedroom overlooking the lake.

"Spiffy," she commented, shaking out my yellow dress with appliquéd daisies and hanging it in the closet. "You can wear it to the party tonight."

I yawned. "What party?"

She picked up another garment. "Mother thought it would be a good idea to have some friends in to meet you. So you'd get to know people and start feeling comfortable right away."

"Oh. But I thought–"

"Thought what?"

"I thought we'd–you know–" I didn't know exactly what I thought. But I knew it involved only Maisie and me, and not a bunch of other people.

She giggled. "You're too tired to string two thoughts together. I'll let you get a bath and some rest. I'll wake you in time for dinner."

"Okay." I felt the lump in my pocket. "Wait! I almost forgot. I brought you something."

Proudly I produced the glorious marble and held it toward her. She took it and rolled it over in her hand.

"Thank you. It's pretty."

"Feel how heavy it is," I urged. "It's a top-notch shooter. Sammy Wardlow's pride and joy, until I made him fork it over. Boy, was he ever steamed when I yelled 'keepsies'!"

I waited for her to congratulate me. She looked at me as if I were speaking Swahili.

I sucked in a breath. "Anyway, I knew you'd like it."

"I do." She turned it so it sparkled. "It's a beaut. I'll keep it right here on the dresser, where it will catch the light."

Catch the light? "It's–it's for playing with." Did I really have to explain?

She shot me a sidelong glance. "At our high school, only boys play with marbles."

My face grew hot. "Oh, piffle. What do the girls do?"

"This and that." She gave a little shrug. "Play cribbage, mostly. And talk about the boys."

I stared at her, unsure of what to say. Disappointment washed over me. This was going to be one long summer, if all we could do was play cribbage and talk about boys.

She set the marble next to a framed photo.

"Who's that?" I pointed.

Maisie blushed. "That's Herbert."

Sensing we were entering strange and unfamiliar territory, I proceeded with caution.

"Who's he?"

Her color deepened. "A boy at school. I think he's the bee's knees, but he never even notices me. As far as he's concerned, I blend with the wallpaper."

"Then he's a dope." A good-looking dope, I had to admit. Although his ears stuck out a little.

"You have your rest now," she said quickly. "You'll find clean towels next to the tub."

Too flagged to argue, I soaked in the immaculate claw-footed tub, put on fresh underthings, and crawled into Maisie's bed.

When I awoke, dazed and disoriented, the setting sun slanted through the window.

"Get out of bed, sleepyhead." Maisie chirped as she set a tray on the nightstand. "You were sleeping so soundly that Mother didn't want to disturb you for dinner. She sent up a sandwich and a glass of milk instead. But now you'd better get changed. Our guests will be arriving any minute."

I sat up and nibbled the ham sandwich while Maisie bustled around the room, chatting about this or that person who'd be at the party.

"Margaret's father works with Dad at the mill. She lives three doors down."

"Will Sir Herbert the Sublime be there?"

"Yes, but you mustn't let on that I like him. I'd be mortified."

"Mum's the word." I noticed she'd changed into a sophisticated lilac-colored sheath decorated with beaded swirls, and a matching headband worn low across her forehead. I sighed at the thought of my yellow daisy dress, in all its Midwestern earnestness. But after I was dressed, she pinned my hair in a way that made it look bobbed, if you didn't peer too closely. She also lent me a bit of lip rouge. I smiled at the mirror. What Frances didn't know wouldn't hurt her.

Downstairs the doorbell rang. "Let's get a wiggle on," Maisie said, and off we went.

The next couple hours passed in a blur. We sipped punch, and Maisie introduced me around. When the dancing started, I mostly stood by, changing records on the Victrola and watching Maisie turkey-trot with one fellow after another, none of whom was Herbert. What was the matter with that goof? Couldn't he see Maisie was the cat's meow?

Finally, bored and feeling like a canceled stamp, I escaped the muggy parlor and wandered out to the porch. Moonlight spilled over the lawn and glittered on Lake Coeur d'Alene. I breathed in the refreshing pine-scented air.

At one end of the porch, under an electric light, a group of boys knelt in a circle, playing marbles. Suddenly my shooting finger itched. I walked over to them.

"Hey, can I play?"

The boys glanced up. Herbert said, "Girls don't play marbles."

"Malarkey. Says who?"

"Aw, let her in," said a boy named Stanley. "She'll probably fizzle out, anyway."

I gathered my skirt and knelt on the plank floor. Stanley lined up a few aggies from his stash and I knuckled down. "We're playing for fair, not for keeps," he said solemnly. I nodded.

After several games in which I'd held my own, a shadow hovered. Glancing over, I recognized Maisie's dancing slippers.

"There you are," she said, hands on hips. "I wondered where you went."

Then she must have noticed Herbert, because her breath caught and fluttered a little. He didn't glance up. I sighed. Clearly my help was needed.

"Maisie," I said, with a meaningful look, "why don't you go upstairs and fetch the present I gave you?" I hoped she'd take the hint. If Herbert wouldn't dance with the girl, the least he could do was let her shoot.

She hesitated, but left and came back, carrying the blue cats-eye, along with a leather pouch full of mibs that must have been tucked away somewhere with other childhood relics.

"Make room." She joined us on the floor.

Herbert's eyes widened when he saw the gleaming cat's-eye. They grew even wider as she handily won game after game.

I grinned. The old Maisie was back.

Later, when I spotted her and Herbert fox-trotting together, my heart sang that a talent for shooting marbles could succeed where lip rouge failed.

I wandered across the dark lawn and found a bench facing toward Lake Coeur d'Alene. Moonlight rippled on the water.

The boy called Stanley appeared out of nowhere.

"May I join you?"

"It's a free country." I shifted over. He folded his lanky body onto the bench, careful not to spill a dish containing a heaping concoction of ice cream, chocolate syrup, and nuts.

"Want some?"

"No, thanks."

We sat in silence for a moment. Then he said, "Gosh, I never met a girl who was good at marbles before."

"Maisie's a whiz," I agreed.

"I meant you."

"Oh."

He cleared his throat. "A bunch of us are going swimming tomorrow. You and Maisie should come." It was more a statement than a question.

"Oh," I said again.

It was going to be a long summer if all I could think of to say was "oh."

He lifted a spoonful of ice cream, held it toward me, and smiled.

Maybe this summer wasn't going to be such a dud, after all.

Trouble Brewing

"I'll get your arm through this sleeve if it's the last thing I do," I muttered through gritted teeth as I wrestled my victim to the carpeted floor of Ladies' Nightwear.

Nothing infuriated me more than a stubborn mannequin, and this one absolutely refused to cooperate. The more I struggled to cloak its celluloid limbs in slippery satin lounging pajamas, the more it balked. Perhaps it didn't care for the look of the garment I was forcing it to wear. Frankly, neither did I.

"I don't care if the color is duller than Lake Michigan in February," I hissed. "You're going to wear it and pretend you like it, or Mrs. Cross will tan my hide."

"Who are you talking to?"

I hadn't heard my friend Dot approach, but I recognized her shoes on the carpet next to me: dainty rose-hued suede pumps fastened with clever grosgrain bows.

"Nobody," I grumped. Dot had it easy. In the Millinery department, they only had to deal with heads. "Say, give me a hand here, will you?"

Dot grasped the mannequin's shoulders and I maneuvered the legs, and soon we had it dressed and standing at the center of Ladies Nightwear, draped in satin the color of lead.

"Come on. Time for lunch." Dot patted her shiny dark bob.

After a brief check-in with my supervisor, Mrs. Cross, I joined Dot on the elevator down to the employee cafeteria of Marshall Field & Company. As we passed through the food line, I glanced quickly around to see if the current object of my affection was anywhere in sight.

"You can stop craning your neck. He won't be down before twelve-thirty," Dot said in a matter-of-fact tone.

"Who?"

She slid me a glance, not buying my innocence routine. "That good-looking manager you're so moony about. He never eats lunch before twelve-thirty. Sometimes not until one."

I felt my face flush. "How do you know what time he eats? Anyway, I'm not moony about him."

She shrugged. "Whatever you say. Come on, Betty's waving us over."

We carried our trays to a crowded table. A couple of women shifted their chairs to make room for us.

"...and the line stretched all the way down the stairs," Agnes-in-Books was saying, between bites of a celery stalk. We clerks tended to identify each other by the sections we worked in, which meant I got stuck with "Marjorie-in-Ladies-Nightwear," much to my embarrassment.

"What line?" I asked as I set down my tray.

"Bess Streeter Aldrich did a book signing of *A Lantern in Her Hand* this morning," she said. "I had no idea she'd draw such a crowd. It will take us all afternoon to recover."

"Oh, I wish I'd known," I said. "My sister Helen simply adored that book. She–"

I was about to pitch in my two cents' worth when I saw Peter Bachmann enter the room, looking snazzy as usual in his crisp white shirt and dark blue tie, and lost my train of thought. He was a walking advertisement for the menswear section he managed, with a tall physique, neat, close-cropped wavy brown hair and hazel eyes (at least I imagined they were hazel; I'd never gotten close enough to tell for sure). My heart gave a little leap, then sank as I watched him choose a table with a gorgeous redhead who worked in Fine Jewelry. When you stacked Fine Jewelry up against Ladies Nightwear, or a tall, beautiful redhead against Marjorie Corrigan, there was no contest in the glamour realm. I might as well have been part of the tastefully subdued wallpaper, for all the notice Peter Bachmann would ever take of me.

When I snapped out of my reverie, the conversation had turned from bestselling authors to Prohibition.

"I tell you, Prohibition is for the birds," Betty-in-Hosiery snapped.

"What about it?" I said, rejoining the conversation. With a stepmother who was president of the WCTU, Kerryville chapter, my family's home was littered with Prohibition literature. I'd been hearing all about the evils of liquor since I was a little tyke.

"Agnes here has been telling us about some goings-on in her neighborhood," Betty said. "Apparently it's become a hotbed of criminal activity."

"It's not that bad," Agnes said. "It's just that the police have been cracking down on bootleggers and home brewers. My next-door neighbor got raided just last week. Turns out he's been operating a still in his basement."

"Prohibition makes scofflaws out of the most law-abiding citizens," Betty protested. "It's simply a colossal failure."

"But don't you think society would be better with liquor removed?" I said.

"But it's not removed," Betty countered. "It's just in the hands of the criminals now. Gangsters are prospering, yet the workingman can't enjoy a drop of his hard-earned beer."

She had a point. Gang warfare was rife on the streets of Chicago and elsewhere, fueled in large part by the underground liquor-smuggling trade. And frankly I didn't think it was fair to arrest people just for brewing beer quietly in their own homes, for their own use. But I was too steeped in the principles of the temperance movement to say it was totally a bad idea–even though it was starting to look that way. I took a bite of my tuna sandwich to give my mouth something better to do than argue.

The rest of the afternoon passed uneventfully. After work, the pleasant spring evening enticed Dot and me to walk home rather than take our usual streetcar. We rented the upper floor of a two-flat on the North Side from a widow lady named Mrs. Moran, who lived on the ground floor.

Even in the heart of the city, springtime scented the air with warm earth and budding blossoms. We took our time walking home, filling our lungs with the clean breath of spring, which turned out to be a good thing, because when we arrived home, the most horrific smell wafted up from Mrs. Moran's apartment, like a combination of wet dog, sauerkraut, and yeast gone bad.

"Good grief, what's that?" I wrinkled my nose in disgust as we entered our apartment.

Dot hurried to the bank of windows that overlooked the street and hoisted them open, one by one. "Mrs. Moran's making her spring tonic," she gasped. "An annual ritual, I'm afraid."

"Spring tonic?"

"She makes it every year. It's some kind of health tonic. She swears by it. Says it keeps her fit as a fiddle. But every year I forget all about it, until I smell that smell."

"Pretty distinct, I must say," I said. "Whew! Let's get the electric fan going."

Several evenings a week, Dot moonlighted as a singer in a "club" (really a speakeasy, though neither of us used that term) called Louie's Villa Italiana, and tonight was one of those nights. For once, I envied her. She got to leave the apartment and breathe normally, while I was stuck home with the smell. It even kept me awake. Finally I could take it no more. I went down to Mrs. Moran's to see if I could convince her to let up for a while.

"Come in, Marjorie," said the jolly white-haired woman when she opened the door in response to my knock. "You're just in time to try my first batch of tonic."

"That's what I came to talk to you about," I said. "The smell is really bad upstairs."

"Don't think of it as bad," she said. "Think of it as the bracing odor of the earth."

Earthworms would be more like it. Rotting ones. But as she showed me the set-up in her kitchen, she explained that the ingredients included a lot of tender wild greens plucked from empty lots and parks.

"I pick them before dawn," she said. "That's when they're at their freshest."

And when the policemen are at their sleepiest, I thought, though I didn't say that out loud. But I did say, "You really shouldn't be roaming the city alone in the dark, Mrs. Moran. Anything could happen."

She fluttered a hand. "Oh, nobody takes any notice of an old woman out picking wildflowers."

"Do you think you could do something about the smell?" I said, getting back to the reason for my visit. "It's really strong upstairs, and makes it hard to sleep."

"Oh, dear, I am sorry about that," she said. "It should be dissipated soon. Meanwhile, why don't you take a bottle with you? A spoonful before bed will help you sleep better. It also purifies the blood, clears up digestive problems, and makes the skin glow." She grinned. "Some say it's even a love potion. Attracts admirers to a person like moths to a lantern."

I accepted a bottle to be polite, barely hiding my skepticism. But I had been feeling a bit poorly lately–sluggish and tired–and I needed to get some sleep. I liked and trusted Mrs. Moran. What harm could it do to take just a spoonful? I held my nose, swallowed, and crawled into bed. Before long, I was fast asleep.

I woke up feeling more cheerful than I had in days. My mood must have shown, because I made a sizeable sale to a sizeable matron who was choosing nightwear to pack for an extended tour of Europe, Even Mrs. Cross was pleased with the morning's tally. However, I was late in taking my lunch hour and had to sit alone. I had just settled in with the comic pages of the *Tribune* when a male voice said,

"Excuse me. Have you finished with the sports section?"

I looked up into the striking hazel (yes) eyes of Peter Bachmann. My heart plummeted to my stomach.

"Sure," I squeaked. "Here."

I rifled through the newspaper and handed him the sports pages. He looked at me with curiosity.

"Are you new here?"

"Not really. I started working here in May." I held out my hand and hoped my palm wasn't sweaty or covered in newspaper ink. "Marjorie Corrigan. Ladies' Nightwear."

He took my hand, and something like an electric charge shot up my arm.

"Peter Bachmann. The Store for Men." He looked puzzled. "Funny, I don't remember ever seeing you before. And I'm sure I would have remembered."

Heat rose in my chest. "Well, Marshall Field's is a big place," I mumbled. I was tempted to say something about redheads from Fine Jewelry holding a person's attention, but thought the better of it.

"Mind if I join you?" he said, pulling out the chair opposite mine.

"Not at all, but–" I checked my wristwatch and swallowed my disappointment. "My break is almost over. I have to get back to Ladies' Nightwear or Mrs. Cross will have a fit."

"Oh." He looked genuinely disappointed. "Well, perhaps I'll see you tomorrow, then? Same time, same place?"

"Sure," I said, standing and lifting my tray. "Tomorrow."

"I'll look for you."

"All right."

On the streetcar ride home from work, I related the whole conversation to Dot.

"It's the darnedest thing," I mused. "He's never so much as glanced my way before."

"Well, I'm not surprised. You're cute as a bug, even if your hat could use a little updating." She eyed my dowdy brown hat with a practiced eye. "We just got in some darling cloches in Millinery. You should try one."

"He doesn't care about my hat," I said. "Let's face it. He probably just wanted the sports pages."

"Oh, don't be such a gloomy Gus." She settled back against the seat. "Anyway, maybe Mrs. Moran was right. Maybe her tonic does give a boost to more than just your blood." She winked at me.

I didn't respond, but that night I held my nose and took an extra spoonful of the tonic, just in case. Again, I slept like a stone, and awoke feeling energetic and bright. So bright, in fact, that before lunch I stopped by the Millinery department and bought a new cloche with the commission from my big sale. Dot pronounced it the perfect complement to my brown hair and eyes.

I looked for Peter Bachmann in the employee lunch room. Sure enough, he was there. He waved me over to his table.

After an enjoyable lunch that sped by way too fast, he said, "Say, Marjorie, I see that the new John Gilbert picture just opened at the State-Lake Theater. Would you care to join me Saturday night?"

Would I ever! A few days later we met up at the employee entrance after work and got better acquainted over chop suey. And the fact that the John Gilbert movie was a war picture filled with bloody battles did not dim my enthusiasm one bit. By the time he saw me home and said good-night, I was walking on air, and I had Mrs. Moran's spring tonic to thank.

As I entered the apartment, I inhaled deeply, and smelled only lilacs from the blossoming tree outside the window. Mrs. Moran was right—either the bad smell had dissipated, or I'd gotten used to it. In either case, I took my nightly slug of Mrs. Moran's tonic and went to bed.

Well past midnight I was jerked from a sound sleep by brilliant flashes of red and blue light that sliced through the window, splashed across the ceiling, and ran down the walls. Heart pounding, I lay back and listened. Late-night traffic stops were not uncommon in our well-traveled neighborhood. But when I heard deep male voices floating up through the radiator pipes from the floor below, I sprang out of bed and grabbed my robe and slippers. This wasn't just some random traffic stop; this was our place!

A quick check confirmed Dot's bed hadn't been slept in. The illuminated dial clock by her bedside read 1:15. She wasn't due home from Louie's until two. I flew down the stairs and found the door to Mrs. Moran's apartment flung wide open.

"Hello? Mrs. Moran?" Cautiously I entered. Splashes of red and blue illuminated the dark living room as I crossed toward the lighted kitchen.

A fair-haired police officer stood with his back to me, blocking the kitchen doorway. Over his shoulder I spotted Mrs. Moran seated at the kitchen table next to an older, gray-haired officer, who jotted notes on a pad as she spoke.

"... and lambs-quarters, and dandelion, and violet, and curly dock, and then the secret ingredient ..." She cleared her throat, leaned over, and murmured something quietly. He nodded and made a note on his pad. She sat back with a look of satisfaction on her face. "So you see? Not one single drop of alcohol. Make sure to put that in your report." She stabbed his notebook with a forefinger.

I nudged the younger officer, who let me pass.

"Mrs. Moran, are you all right?"

She was dressed haphazardly as usual in a faded house dress and flour-sack apron, stray snowy hairs escaping from her bun. When she saw me, her face lit up.

"Marjorie! How good of you to come," she said brightly, as if sitting in her kitchen surrounded by police officers in the middle of the night was an ordinary occurrence.

"What's going on?"

"Of all the ridiculous things," she huffed. "I had just put my last batch of tonic on to stew, minding my own business, when these two officers of the law burst onto my property and tried to haul me off in the middle of the night like a common criminal."

"What on earth–?" I looked to the older officer for some kind of explanation.

"You her daughter?" His voice was gruff.

"Upstairs neighbor. She's my landlady." He scribbled a note onto his pad.

"Terribly sorry for the misunderstanding, miss," the younger officer spoke up. "We got a call down at the station from someone who was quite sure that your landlady here was brewing up moonshine in her kitchen."

With an indignant huff, Mrs. Moran gestured toward the stove, where the tonic-making apparatus stood in a tangle of tubes and vials. "Officer Peterson, can you stand there with a straight face and tell me that that contraption looks anything like a still?"

The younger officer cleared his throat. "Well, to be perfectly honest, ma'am, it surely does."

"Well!" Mrs. Moran lifted her chin. "In any case, Marjorie, I've been explaining to the good officers the profound difference between bootleg whiskey and my good spring tonic. That's Officer Peterson, by the way,"–she pointed to the blond officer–"and this is Officer Stevens."

"How do you do." Suddenly conscious of my disheveled state, I clutched the throat of my robe. "How could this happen?" I glared at young Officer Peterson, who blushed.

"You must admit, miss, that it looks mighty suspicious," gray-haired Officer Stevens said, squinting at the tonic machine. "We don't come across too many widow ladies who operate such unusual manufacturing facilities in their kitchens."

"Well, now you know one," Mrs. Moran said.

Officer Peterson looked sheepish. "Sorry again for the inconvenience, ma'am. It won't happen again."

The older officer stood and snapped his notepad shut. "I think we're done here. Officer Peterson, let's be on our way."

"Just a moment, Officer Stevens," Mrs. Moran said. "Take this with you." She produced a small vial from her apron pocket and handed it to him. "Apply it with a cotton ball, morning and night. That rash on your hand should clear up in no time."

"Thank you, ma'am." He touched the brim of his hat.

As we escorted the officers to the door, the younger one grinned at me, displaying a dimple. "Sorry to have woken you, miss."

I lifted my chin. "No harm done." Policemen had no business having dimples. And I had no business noticing.

Mrs. Moran and I stood at the front window and watched the police cruiser pull away from the curb.

"Who do you think telephoned the police?" I asked.

"Probably that old Mr. Kern from next door. He's been complaining about the smell." We turned away from the window. "For heaven's sake. Moonshine, indeed. Have you ever heard of anything so ridiculous?"

I shrugged. "Maybe it's not moonshine, but I'm pretty sure it's some kind of a love potion. You could make a killing if you sold this stuff."

"Don't be ridiculous," she said. "I was just teasing you with all that love-potion malarkey. All the tonic does is purify your blood and improve your digestion. If proper digestion has something of an aphrodisiac effect, well–" She shrugged. We both laughed and said our good-nights, and I went upstairs and tumbled back into bed.

But a few days later, when an invitation to the policeman's ball arrived in Mrs. Moran's mailbox from a certain silver-haired officer, I wasn't surprised in the least.

Thank You For Reading!

If you enjoyed meeting Dot, Marjorie, and Helen in these short stories, you'll be glad to hear they also appear in a series of Roaring Twenties novels by Jennifer Lamont Leo:

You're the Cream in My Coffee

and

Ain't Misbehavin'

Look for them at your favorite bookseller or online.

ABOUT THE AUTHOR

Jennifer Lamont Leo captures readers' hearts through stories set in times gone by. Her first novel, You're the Cream in My Coffee, won the 2017 ACFW Carol Award for debut novel, as well as a Grace Award for women's fiction. In additional to writing fiction, Jennifer is a freelance writer, a copywriter, and an editor.

She lives in northern Idaho with her husband, two cats, and abundant wildlife.

Sign up for Jennifer's reader community to receive notice of new novels and other stories, giveaways, and other goodies at JenniferLamontLeo.com, and follow Jennifer on Facebook, Twitter, and Pinterest..